BODY IN A BARREL

A LAS VEGAS MAFIA CRIME NOVELLA

AARON MEAD

PRESS TOGETHER

The Library of Congress has catalogued the Press Together edition as follows:

Names: Mead, Aaron, author.

Title: Body in a Barrel / Aaron Mead

Description: First edition | Los Angeles : Press Together, 2025.
Library of Congress Control Number: 2025912880 (print)
Press Together Trade Paperback ISBN: 979-8-9992206-0-8
ebook ISBN: 979-8-9992206-1-5
Cover design by Nick Castle

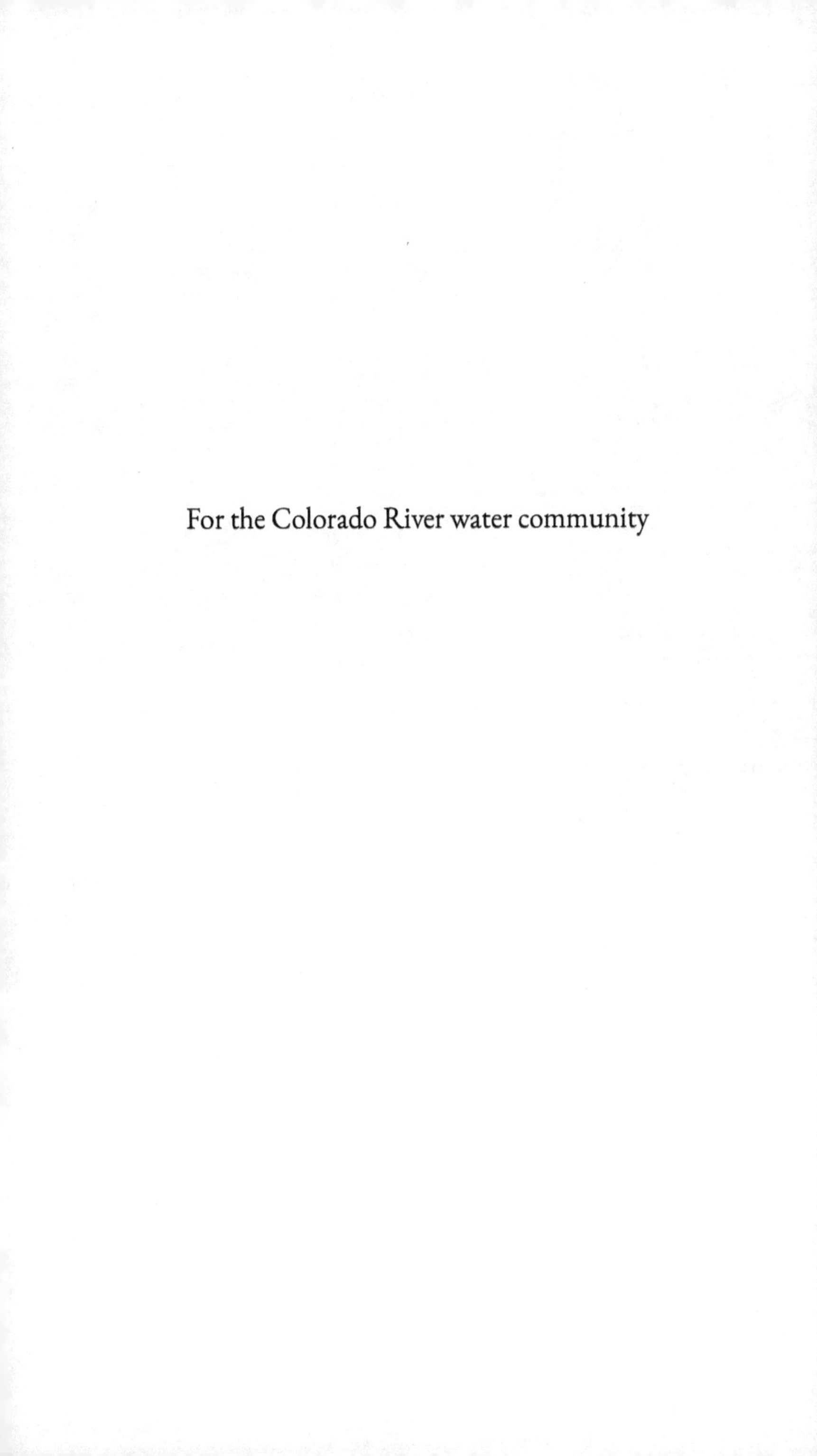

For the Colorado River water community

1

L ENNY SIPPED INSTANT COFFEE spiked with whiskey and scratched his gut through the hole in his pajamas. Afternoon heat radiated from the flimsy walls of the mobile home. He'd slept little again. Always the same nightmare: a faceless man with a hammer chasing him down a dark hallway. His head ached. He felt like a sponge, wrung out and left to dry.

As he ran a shaky hand across the front page of the Las Vegas Review Journal, which lay on his tiny kitchen table, he took another desperate sip from the mug. A headline read, "More human remains found at Lake Mead." This time, just bones, scattered on the shore at Callville Bay. Likely a drowning. Since the year before, the reservoir had dropped like a bad stock, baring long-hidden contents on spreading mud beaches. The papers said this was the new reality: a hotter, drier climate, with less water flowing to the lake from upstream. But Lenny suspected the Californians were sucking up all the water downstream.

The week before, the lake had surrendered the Hemenway Harbor Doe, the body wearing Trax velcro sneakers and nylon parachute pants from Kmart, preserved in a barrel, bullet hole in the head. Since reading last week's article, Lenny had waffled over whether to check the second barrel. Last night, over his fourth double Jack Daniel's, he'd made up his mind.

He glanced at yesterday's mail beside the paper: just junk, the top piece from climate activists seeking donations. How was he on their mailing list? Probably Carol's doing. She'd loved cats; they'd had three when she was around. One sprayed in the corner of their tiny living room on the puke-green shag, and though she'd moved out fifteen years ago, it still smelled on hot days. She donated once to an animal shelter, and the mailers never stopped. Requests from wildlife groups followed and now the climate change wackos.

He rose from the table, finished his coffee, and introduced his cup to the dirty jumble on the counter. As he ducked his head to avoid the bedroom doorframe, he clenched and unclenched his jaw. Shower? Why bother when it's so damned hot? He dressed in yesterday's clothes: a once-white button-up with a formless collar and permanent armpit stains, brown polyester slacks that rode under his belly, black socks with tired elastic, and a black belt matching his polished shoes—both Italian leather.

Vince Bonucci's father, Tony, had given Lenny the shoes and belt when he started working for him in 1978. He was seventeen then . . . and lost. Lenny's dad had worked the cashier's cage at the Stardust, on the payroll of the Outfit. When Lenny was a freshman at Bishop Gorman Catholic, they sent his dad to L.A., and within weeks he got arrested, ending up in the Victorville Pen. That's when Lenny started punching. First it was the kids making fun of his jailbird pop. A few black eyes stopped the teasing, but he kept going. Something about his fist against a face just felt right. He went for the big egos; football players were his favorite. At six-four and two hundred and seventy pounds, Lenny was imposing. His limbs were thick hairy tubes, not cut and pretty, but back then, strong as hell under the masking layer of fat. A cocky quarterback from California picked on Vince, which nobody did. Unless you didn't know his dad. So Lenny clocked the idiot, nose against knuckles, blood everywhere. The Bonuccis invited him over.

He'd loved the Bonuccis' house. The aqua pool, shimmering like a jewel in the sunlight, the sprawling concrete deck, even some grass—back before pools and lawns were endangered species in Vegas. Vince's mom stirred Lenny's teenage hormones, lounging on the pool deck in a bikini, and her meatballs tasted like love. Tony had been his second father: he just *got* Lenny, that special mix of sad and angry. Mostly angry. With Lenny's dad in prison and his mom the only earner—a cocktail waitress at the Stardust—they lost their house and moved to the trailer park. Still the debts piled up. Near the end of sophomore year, when Lenny found his mom dead in the back bedroom, empty pill bottle on the bedside table, the Bonuccis took him in. Two months before graduation, Tony offered him the job, and Lenny dropped out.

2

THE CHEAP ALUMINUM DOOR clattered shut as Lenny stepped outside, submerging in the hot air. A faint smoke smell tickled his nostrils, and a dog barked in the distance. He scowled at his neighbors' melting fake lawn. It was May, and Christmas lights still looped below their decaying eaves. The plastic thermometer hanging from a nail in the siding read 115 degrees.

He backed his rusty pickup toward the boat (his father's only bequest, apart from debts), got out, and burned his hand on the sun-hot metal of the trailer while attaching the hitch. He got back in the cab, gripped the wheel with still-stinging hands, and guided the truck out the potholed driveway, boat in tow. As he headed west on Tropicana, an apocalyptic mushroom cloud bloomed in the orange sky, like someone dropped an A-bomb on Charleston Peak.

In fact, it was smoke from the wildfires he'd read about yesterday.

Forty minutes later, he passed through Boulder City, paid the entry fee at the park entrance kiosk, and wound his way down to Hemenway Harbor. Lake Mead appeared. Moon rocks in burnt sienna and battleship gray set the familiar horizon above the water, but the chalk-white bathtub ring and the archipelago of bleached islands, left by the receding water, looked alien.

In the late sixties, when his dad took him fishing, the lake was up over 1100 feet. "Used to be higher," he'd tell him, trying to impress. In 1999, it was over 1200 feet and virtually full, but Y2K was a turning point. The computers did fine, as Lenny recalled; the lake did not. It began a halting decline they called the "millennium drought." Too little snow in Colorado, too much cattle-feed in California, and that relentless desert heat sucking six feet of lake into thin air, year upon year. As Lenny rumbled down the concrete boat ramp, he could barely see the shoreline half a mile farther out than when he'd been there last. With Tony's guy Frank.

Lenny had started as Tony's errand boy. He got coffee, ran messages between casinos, and drove stuff around the city—drills, crowbars, lock picks, sometimes guns and ammo. After a few months, Tony sent him to watch homes of delinquent clients: alcoholic gamblers missing their weekly vig, small-time street dealers dodging protection payments. Soon watching clients led to threatening them, and Lenny was back to breaking noses. After a year diligently applying himself, he graduated to wheelman for Tony's gang of burglars. A few months more and he drove for contract hits, which entailed helping bury bodies in the desert. Putting them in barrels and dumping them in the lake had been Lenny's invention. Casino food services trashed multiple barrels each week—filled with flour or butter on the way in, empty on the way out—so they were easy enough to get. Tony's hitmen loved the new method: no digging. Tony also thought it was clever. What Lenny hadn't foreseen was Tony's suggestion he start helping with the hits. Tony sold the work like a golden ticket, his face nearly gleeful: "One hit and you're good as made." But Lenny wasn't so sure.

The first hit, he only watched as Frank whacked a greedy collector for Tony's loan sharking operation. Frank was Tony's boyhood friend from Chicago. He looked like an ordinary middle-aged guy—bell-bottom business slacks, wide-collared polyester polos, snakeskin derbies, slight beer belly, graying mat of combed-over hair, and glasses thick enough to stop bullets. But make no mistake—Frank was professional. Lenny stood in the hallway of the collector's apartment while Frank dropped him with a single shot to the head. Tidy. Efficient. They packed him in the drum right there in the hallway and carried him out to the boat trailer like a barrel of diced tomatoes. Lenny thought they dumped him too close to shore, but Frank was tired, his wife wanted him home, and they hadn't foreseen the reservoir's shriveled future.

On his way down the ramp, Lenny passed signs that marked the dropping lake level, year-by-year—2000, 2002, 2008, 2018, 2021. He neared the spot where they'd dumped the first barrel and came to a stop. Crime-scene tape still marked it off, but there were no cops, just some idiot walking his dog in the blistering heat. A bead of sweat cut loose from the cluster on Lenny's bald head and trickled between his eyes, down the side of his nose. The air conditioner in the truck was anemic. The idea to fix it flashed through his mind, but he knew he wouldn't. The dog trailed a leash-length behind its person, tongue lolling like a dead fish. He felt sorry for it. He opened his mouth wide to stretch the muscles, and his jaw clicked like a tap shoe.

Near the shoreline, Lenny turned the rig around and backed the trailer down the last twenty yards of ramp, sinking the back wheels in the water beside the floating dock. Reaching into the glove box to retrieve a small flashlight, he noticed the pint-bottle of Jack Daniel's beside his wallet. He unscrewed the cap, took a swallow, replaced it, and clipped the flashlight to his belt. He left the cab and cranked the winch handle with a shaky hand so the boat eased from the trailer, into the water. The breeze off the lake felt like a hair dryer blowing in his face. His heart beat in his throat.

After parking the truck and trailer, Lenny got in the boat and pushed off from the dock with a long-handled gaff. He flipped the four-horse Evinrude into the water, squeezed the primer bulb, adjusted the trim, yanked the cord three, four, five times, and took in the comforting smell of fuel as the vintage outboard coughed to life. Puttering out fifty yards, around the breakwater, he idled the engine and drifted into deeper water.

In 1979, when the lake was high, they'd dumped the second barrel in 150 feet of water. Now the bed was a mere eight feet below, and objects on the bottom were easy to see: a clump of stargrass, rocks, a log. Lenny squinted at Big Boulder Island—now joined with Little Boulder and Rock Islands, the masses having merged as the lake dropped. He tried to recall how it looked that night, the moonlit angles, the perspective. It seemed the right distance, but it was hard to tell. Back then, he'd looked across at the islands; now he looked up at them. The band of white around their shoreline called to mind bare buttocks.

He refocused on the water near the boat, scanning back and forth, peering into the depths, his jaw tight again. Too far now. Ramping up the motor, he began a new transect twenty feet farther along the shore. The sun neared the horizon. Five more transects and Lenny felt desperation twinge in his belly. Where dammit? He motored back toward the dock and started again, his chest tightening. Finally, after three more passes, his eye caught a dark curve, a submerged circle camouflaged by thick stargrass swaying in the currents. He exhaled through puffed cheeks. Lenny maneuvered the boat closer and idled the engine. As he gazed through the water at the steel barrel, a round stain on the lake bed, a door inside him unlocked and swung open.

The second hit had been Lenny's. The Las Vegas police flipped a valet at the Flamingo—a guy who used to tip off Tony to the whereabouts of rich guests at the hotel-casino, from whom Tony's gang then stole wads of cash and jewelry. The valet was scheduled to testify, so his time had come. Frank joined him the night of the hit, but Tony assigned the business to Lenny. "Good as made," he'd said again. They'd lost the silencer, so Frank had broken the bullets into half-loads, removing gun powder from the shells for a quieter kill. They confronted the valet in his home, and when he ran, Lenny shot him and shot him, but he wouldn't fall. First his shoulder, then his leg, then, when he'd slowed, his head, but he just wouldn't go. They chased him into the garage. Lenny was out of bullets, so Frank passed him a hammer. His hands shook so much he could barely slide the blood-slick body into the barrel. They repeated the lake disposal, but this time Lenny insisted they dump it farther out. He couldn't sleep for a week, and after that only—and barely—with whiskey.

Lenny stared through the water. A panicky tremor began in his hands, and he could smell his armpits. The barrel was too shallow, he thought. Way too shallow. And how much more would the lake drop? He grabbed the gaff in his vibrating hands, stood it upright beside the boat, and then lowered it toward the barrel, trying to snag the drum rim with the hook. His first efforts caught only stargrass. He managed to hook the rim but had no leverage from the middle of the boat. He shifted to the stern. As he jerked at the gaff, trying to move the barrel deeper, the boat drifted back toward shore while the barrel stayed put.

The sun set, an overfried egg yolk devoured by the craggy horizon, the air still aflame. Sweat rolled through the drenched band of Lenny's gray hair, soaking into his collar. In the dying light, through the surface ripples, amidst the stargrass, the circular top of the barrel looked like a face. Red lettering on the boat reflected in the water. A bloody face, stretching and shifting like a funhouse mirror. The valet's terrified face as he flees down the hallway, half-strength bullets lodged in his body, his mouth pleading as he stumbles and falls on the polished concrete. A broken, empty face once he yields and Lenny sets down the hammer.

He blinked, trying for a different image, while his heart battered his ribcage. He shook the gaff, but the barrel wouldn't budge. After maneuvering so the barrel was just off the stern, he relatched the hook onto the rim, gripped the gaff tight in his right hand, and cranked the trim with his left. The engine revved, and the boat lurched away from shore. Suddenly, Lenny was leaning over the stern, hook locked onto the rim, right hand fixed to the gaff like a tree root clutching rocky soil. Still the barrel held. The Evinrude spluttered then surged, and Lenny felt his weight shift farther over the transom. He seized the gaff with his second hand and growled, his eyes wide and watery. The barrel finally budged. As it tilted and dropped to its side on a bed of stargrass, Lenny lost his balance and fell in. Freed from its anchor, the boat motored into the spreading darkness.

As he plunged downward, Lenny opened his mouth and took the lake into his lungs. The gaff handle had threaded through his cuff and out the gap between cuff and first button; with the hook still locked to the rim, he found himself upside down in the dark water, tethered to the barrel. He panicked, thrashing and yanking at the gaff, but it held fast. Another mouthful of water. Was this how he'd go, laid out beside his victim? With a final surge of adrenaline, he wrenched his cuff and burst the button, freeing himself from the gaff. As he pushed off the bed toward the surface, a mere half-shade lighter than the surrounding watery darkness, he kicked the barrel, which sounded like a muted hammer blow. Stargrass felt like hands, clutching, clawing him back to the depths.

He surfaced, coughing and gasping. His ears detected the boat, now two hundred yards out, escaping toward the naked islands. No catching it now. He swam for shore, dizzy, still panicky. His head felt like an overfull balloon.

He reached the truck in darkness, put a hand on the hood, and doubled over, his breathing wild. From across the water, he could hear the four-horse Evinrude still puttering and shook his head. He dug keys from his saturated pants pocket and negotiated the keyhole using the flashlight hooked to his belt—amazed it still worked. He sat stunned in the cab, staring out the windshield and up the dark boat ramp, listening to water drip on the vinyl seat.

3

L ENNY WOKE WITH A start. The sun pierced the windshield like hot needles on his forehead, and the truck cab felt like a preheating oven. He checked his watch. Water slipped over the dial under the glass, the hands frozen at seven forty-five. Memories of the night before flooded back.

He left the truck and walked to the shoreline, socks still wet inside his shoes. Shielding his eyes with his hand and squinting through the daylight, he scanned the islands but saw no boat. His mouth tasted bad, and his stomach grumbled. He looked over at the marina. There'd be a store with food.

He opened the glove box, brushed his wallet aside, and pulled out the bottle of Jack Daniel's. After rinsing his mouth with whiskey, he swallowed and started the truck.

He drove back up the furrowed ramp, empty trailer chattering like teeth, and headed for the marina parking lot.

As he walked up the ramp onto the dock, he noticed a white Ford Explorer parked just yards away. Swiveling spotlights protruded near the side mirrors, and a black push bar imprisoned the bumper. Two men with mustaches, aviator shades, and tan coats sat in the front seats, tracking his progress. Definitely cops, he thought. He quickened his step.

Outside the marina store, a rail-thin Asian man in shades and a bucket hat leaned back in a plastic chair, mouth open, snoring. An empty malt liquor bottle lay beside the chair.

Lenny's stomach made angry sounds as he stepped inside. A pudgy Asian girl with short blue hair and a Misfits t-shirt sat behind the counter, Doc Martens crossed on the countertop. She looked up from her magazine and eyed Lenny, chewing gum with her mouth open. The place was a riot of neon: glowing orange life vests, pink plastic sunglasses, lurid yellow sun hats, and flashy blue candy. The fluorescent scene taxed his eyes more than the midday sunlight.

Seven flavors of instant noodles lined the food aisle. Lenny picked chicken and held it up to the girl at the counter, who was still watching him. "Hot water?"

"Back there. Two bucks."

"Two bucks?" said Lenny. The noodles were only a dollar forty-nine.

The girl went back to her magazine.

Lenny peeled back the foil lid on the styrofoam cup, poured in the water, plunged a plastic fork into the mixture, and smoothed the lid back over the cup. He grabbed a chocolate bar from the candy aisle and walked to the counter. "Hear anything about a boat this morning?"

The girl set the magazine on her lap, her face amused. "It's a marina, man. Everyone talks about boats."

"Aluminum. Fourteen-footer. Old motor."

The girl stared at him, no longer amused, gum crackling between her jaws.

"Lost my boat last night."

She shrugged. "You gonna buy these?"

Lenny nodded. Some attitude, he thought.

She punched at the cash register, boots still on the counter. "Four forty-eight," she said between chews, her expression now bored.

Lenny felt for his wallet. Still in the truck. "Shit," he said under his breath. "Wallet's in my truck. Be right back." Lenny turned for the door, cup and bar in his hands.

"Nope," said the girl. "Leave it here."

"I'll be right back," said Lenny, his voice leaning toward a whine.

"Leave it," she said with surprising authority, taking her boots off the counter.

Lenny rolled his eyes, shook his head, and set the two items on the counter. "I'll be right back."

When he arrived back at the store with his wallet, the door was locked. He peered through the window. The noodles and candy bar still sat on the counter, but the girl was gone. He pulled back and noticed a sign stuck inside the glass: Back in 10 Minutes.

"What the hell." He looked around. The man in the lawn chair continued to snore. Lenny sighed and leaned against the wall.

After more than ten minutes, the girl hadn't returned. Lenny's stomach complained. He walked farther into the marina, passing docked boats and empty slips. Around a corner and up ahead, he spotted a white fishing boat with four matching motors, gleaming in the sunlight. In the slip beside it, the girl sat in a small aluminum boat, removing the engine. As he got closer, he saw the boat was his. "Hey!"

The girl looked up, suspending her wrench over the motor. She took him in and then went back to her work.

Lenny quickened his stride. "That's my boat!"

She looked up again, her face annoyed.

He arrived at the slip where she was floating. "You stealing my motor?"

"*Yours*?" she said, skeptical.

"I just told you about it!" said Lenny, exasperated. "What's wrong with you?"

She narrowed her eyes at him.

"That's my boat!" Lenny moved for the painter to pull the boat toward the dock.

The girl reached behind her, drawing a pistol from her waistband. "Nope."

Lenny dropped the painter. "Whoa, whoa, whoa. Okay, okay." He put his hands at shoulder height. "Take it easy."

"Don't tell me what to do," said the girl.

"Okay, okay." Lenny stepped back, hands still up.

"That's better." The girl tucked the gun back in her waistband, fierce eyes locked on Lenny. "You done?"

Lenny lowered his hands. "You're in my boat," he said, irritated.

"Prove it."

Lenny sighed and rolled his eyes. "Really? I told you I lost a boat just like that."

She stared at him, unmoved.

Lenny huffed. "You find it out there?" He gestured with his thumb toward Big Boulder Island. "On the shoreline?"

The girl squinted at him. "People find boats all the time around here."

"How'd you get it?"

She pointed to the fishing boat beside her.

"That's yours?" said Lenny. He registered the lights and a steel cable with a six-inch metal hook wound around a motorized winch at the bow.

"Dad's."

Lenny nodded. "I need my boat back."

"Show me the title."

Lenny shook his head and rolled his eyes again. "The empty trailer's on my truck." He gestured toward the parking lot.

"Lotsa trailers around here."

"Oh come on!" Lenny started toward the painter again, but the girl re-drew the handgun.

"The title," she said again.

Reflexively, Lenny stepped back and put his hands in the air once more. His cheeks flashed hot. "Come on. This is ridiculous. What are you, like sixteen?" He put his hands down. "You're not gonna shoot me."

"I'm twenty-three," said the girl, holding the gun steady.

"Well you look like you're sixteen," said Lenny.

"Fuck you."

"You ever fired that thing? Even once?"

She adjusted her grip on the gun.

Lenny yelled at her, "You gonna fuckin' shoot me?" He put his arms high in the air, elbows locked, and stepped toward the boat again. "I'm not doing any-thing, and you're gonna gun me down?"

"Fuck you." Her voice wavered.

Lenny put his hands down. "Put it away," he said, shaking his head. "This is stupid. Give me my boat, or I'm calling the cops."

"Go ahead," she said, still watching him across the gun barrel. "They're gonna want the title too."

Lenny sighed and looked out at the ring around the lake. "It'll take me a few hours."

4

ENNY WOLFED INSTANT NOODLES as he rolled toward the city, styrofoam cup between his legs, one hand on the steering wheel, plastic fork in the other, hot wind from the open window splattering tepid water and oil on his slacks with each bite. When he'd finished the noodles and the candy bar, his mind drifted.

He was glad he'd found his boat, but the girl was crazy. Not nearly as tough as she thought, but still scary, waving that gun around. Her boat, though. Her boat was amazing. The lights. The winch. The engines. If anything could handle a barrel in a lake, it was that boat. It seemed like an ocean rig, equipped for marlin, even though the biggest fish in the lake were striped bass and catfish. But it didn't matter why she had the thing. The point was it could move the barrel.

He arrived back at the marina in the afternoon, boat title tucked in the front pocket of his too-tight slacks. The man in the lawn chair and the malt liquor bottle were gone, but the store was still locked. The sign hung inside the window once again: Back in 10 Minutes.

Lenny made his way down the dock toward the slip where she'd been before and found his boat, still parked beside hers, but it was now chained to the dock, and the Evinrude was missing. "What the fuck," said Lenny, under his breath.

He looked around. A row of three single-story aluminum buildings shaped like half-rolls sat across from the slips, each one with a windowless door. They looked like small warehouses. Lenny tried the handle on the first door, but it was locked. He walked down to the second, and the knob turned. He stepped through into a large room where exposed bulbs hung from the arched ceiling, casting weak light over half a dozen tables, covered and surrounded by boat engines in various states of disrepair, along with an assortment of used parts and tools. The place looked like an outboard junkyard.

The girl stood at a table near the back, under one of the hanging bulbs, working on an engine. She didn't notice Lenny.

"Where's my outboard?" he said.

She startled and looked up, eyes wide. She put down her tool, came out from behind the table, and walked toward him with purpose. "You can't be in here," she said, waving her hands and shooing him toward the door.

Lenny stood his ground. "Where's my motor?"

"Out!" she yelled and continued waving her hands. "We'll talk on the dock."

Lenny sighed and stepped back through the door. She followed him and pulled the door closed, locking the deadbolt with a key.

"Title?" she said, scowling at him.

Lenny dug the paper from his pocket.

She plucked it from his hand and crossed the dock to his boat.

"Hey!" said Lenny.

"Gotta check it," said the girl without looking at him. She scanned the registration number and tags on the aluminum hull and then examined the document. She looked up at him. "Leonardo Battaglia? What the hell kind of name is that?"

"Lenny. It's Italian."

"Lenny?" Her chuckle had a derisive edge. "You should be in a gangster movie."

"Where's my motor," said Lenny for the third time, losing patience.

She nodded sideways toward the aluminum building. "It's broken. Fuel pump's fried."

That checked out, thought Lenny. It must have gone aground and run full-throttle till the tank was dry.

"I can fix it," she said. "Two hundred bucks, parts and labor."

"Two hundred? No way. I can get a fuel pump for twenty-five bucks."

"A shitty one," she said. "And you know how to install it?"

She was squeezing him. She couldn't steal the engine, so now she'd just overcharge to repair it. Lenny didn't answer.

"Take it or leave it," she said.

He thought for a moment. "Where'd you get all the parts?" He tilted his head toward the warehouse.

"Here and there," she said. Her face gave him nothing.

"One fifty," said Lenny. "No more."

"Wait here," she said. "I'll get your broken engine." She turned back to the door and began digging for the keys in her pocket.

He'd need to take it somewhere else, he thought. Probably save fifty bucks at most, and it was worth fifty just to avoid lugging it around. "Okay, okay," he said. "Two hundred."

"Cash," she said. "Come back tomorrow."

"I work tomorrow," said Lenny. "Day after?"

"Not before noon," she said. "I'll be in the store."

Lenny nodded and turned his attention to the gleaming white boat beside his. "So this is yours?"

"Like I said, my dad's."

"He ever rent it out?"

"No. But we take people out in it. Well, I do. Sometimes. If the price is right."

Lenny nodded. "Day after tomorrow," he said and started down the dock toward his truck.

5

THE NEXT DAY, LENNY arrived late to the dump, hung over. As he drove the bulldozer, smoothing mountains of garbage, tearing open trash bags that spilled stinking food waste and endless plastic packaging, grinding them under the machine's hungry tank treads, he thought of the girl's boat. On his lunch break, he called around to boat shops, but nobody rented a rig like hers—one with lights and a big winch.

The following afternoon, Lenny returned to the marina. The unmarked police vehicle was again parked near the dock. As he approached the ramp, the driver-side window buzzed down, and the mustached cop leaned out. He waved Lenny over.

Lenny stopped and gestured toward himself, eyebrows raised, as if not sure it was him the cop wanted.

The cop nodded and waved at him again. When Lenny arrived at the vehicle, the cop flashed his badge. "Detective Green, Boulder City Police."

Lenny churned inside.

"What's your business at the marina today?"

"Seeing a friend." Lenny's words tumbled out, unmeasured.

"You've been around last couple of days." The cop's eyes hid behind his mirrored shades. "Looks like you have a boat in the marina," he said, pointing at the trailer behind Lenny's truck. "Thought you said you were seeing a friend."

Lenny felt his armpits sweating. "My friend's helping me with my boat."

The cop stared at him. "Any problems with missing items?"

"What do you mean?" said Lenny.

"Like parts. Engine parts."

Lenny gave him a confused look. "Engine parts?"

"Yeah. There's been some reports. Know anything about that?"

"No," said Lenny.

The cop stared at him again.

"Yeah, no, nothing like that," said Lenny, fidgeting with his fingers.

The cop looked at him for a few more seconds and then dug out a card and handed it to him. "If you get any helpful information, give me a call."

The window buzzed up, and Lenny turned back toward the dock ramp, heading for the store. The Back in 10 Minutes sign hung inside the window again, so he continued toward the boat slip and the warehouse buildings. His boat was still there, but the girl wasn't outside, so he tried the door where he'd found her last time. It was locked, so he beat on it with the butt of his fist.

After a minute, the deadbolt turned, and the girl poked her head out the door. She looked annoyed. "You bring the cash?"

He nodded.

Still half-inside, she held out her hand and rubbed her thumb against her index and middle fingers.

Lenny pulled out a hundred-dollar bill, and handed it to her.

She tilted her head, her annoyance increasing. "We said two-hundred, Leonardo."

"Well, seeing as how you fixed it with stolen parts, the price has gone down."

"Fuck you, the parts aren't stolen," she said. "Two hundred, or I keep your motor."

"One hundred, or I turn your ass in," said Lenny. "Met two cops on my way in here. Detectives." Lenny pulled the card from his pocket and flashed it. "With a phone number." He paused for effect. "Seems there've been reports of missing engine parts. Bet they'd like to know about your little workshop."

The girl narrowed her eyes. She took the bill. "Asshole," she said under her breath, then withdrew into the building. A few minutes later she reemerged with the motor and brushed past Lenny toward his boat. She reinstalled it, undid the chain, and, without a word, started back toward the aluminum building.

"Hey," said Lenny, gesturing toward her father's boat. "How much to rent it."

"I already told you, we don't rent it out," she said.

"I'm special." Lenny flashed a triumphant smile.

She rolled her eyes and huffed. "Look, I'm not gonna let an old guy who ghost-rides his dinghy onto beaches in the middle of the night rent my boat. I'll take you out fishing, but you gotta pay."

"How much?"

"One fifty an hour."

"Seems like a lot," said Lenny. "How 'bout for your special customers?" His smile returned.

She clenched her jaw. "You know how much gas costs for that thing?"

"One twenty-five," said Lenny.

"Minimum two hours," said the girl.

"Done," said Lenny. "Tonight?"

The girl sighed. "Seven. At the store."

Lenny climbed into his boat. He pulled the engine cord, and it started on the first try. He tipped his head in exaggerated thanks.

She folded her arms.

He backed the boat out of the slip, turned it, and puttered toward the marina entrance.

6

L ENNY ARRIVED OUTSIDE THE marina store just before seven. The sun neared the horizon, but the air
still felt like exhaust from a jet engine. The thin Asian man
again sat in his lawn chair, this time awake. Lenny nodded to him, but he didn't respond. He lifted a half-empty
forty-ounce bottle to his lips and drank.

The girl emerged from the store, acknowledged Lenny,
and then turned to the man in the chair. "Dad."

Again the man didn't respond.

"Dad," she said, this time louder.

The man looked up through glazed eyes.

"I'm taking the boat out," she said.

The liquid in her father's bottle sloshed as he raised it in
a gesture of permission or resignation, Lenny couldn't tell
which.

Arriving at the flashy fishing boat, she turned to face him. "Cash."

Lenny pulled two hundreds and a fifty from his wallet. "Two hours'll be enough."

The girl unhooked the bow line from a small horn cleat, and held it taut. "Get on," she said.

Lenny obeyed. Two fishing rods leaned against the stern near a tackle box on the floor. "What's your name?" he said.

"Wouldn't you like to know," said the girl and scowled at him. She followed him onto the boat, tossed the bow line, and slipped into the driver's seat in the center console. Lenny slumped into the seat beside her, bouncing his knee as if driving a pedal boat. The girl eyed his knee, and Lenny stilled it. He swallowed, staring straight ahead.

She turned the ignition key, and the four engines rumbled like a storm. As she navigated the marina, he eyed a boat beyond the breakwater and recognized the silver cab and orange hull of a Coast Guard vessel. His stomach fluttered. It was heading for the marina. They rounded the breakwater, and the Coast Guard boat passed them thirty yards away. The wake hit them broadside, rocking their boat in and out of wave troughs. The girl accelerated, heading for open water.

"Hold up," said Lenny, raising his hand, watching the Coast Guard boat enter the marina.

She eased off the engines and looked at him, puzzled.

"Slowly," he said. He moved to the front of the boat and leaned over the bow, directing her to the spot where he'd been the night before. His stomach churned.

"What?" she shouted over the engines.

Lenny ignored the question and directed her with his arms. After two short passes, he spotted the barrel on the lake bed, still tipped on its side, the gaff lying beside it. It looked shallower. "Okay! Here!"

She threw the outboards briefly in reverse and then cut them.

"Anchor," said Lenny.

The girl dropped a small anchor off the stern and turned back to Lenny. "There's no fish here. It's too shallow."

"Lower the cable," said Lenny, removing the hook from the winch so it dangled over the side of the boat.

"What the hell?"

"Just do it!" Lenny's heart pumped in his ears.

She shook her head, retook her seat in the console, and flipped a switch. The winch began to turn, dropping the hook into the water.

Lenny let the cable slide through his hands, directing the hook toward the barrel. "Okay, whoa! Slower," he said.

The girl slowed the winch speed.

"Okay! That's it!"

She turned off the winch and looked at him with suspicion.

Lenny put both hands on the cable and tried to maneuver the hook onto the barrel lip. The light had faded, so he couldn't see his target well. He unclipped the small flashlight from his belt and shined it into the water, but the light didn't penetrate far enough. "Bow lights," he said, reclipping the flashlight.

The girl flipped another switch, and a bank of lights projected into the water. While Lenny continued to maneuver the hook, the girl moved to the front of the boat. "What the hell are you doing?" she said as she arrived at the bow.

Lenny kept tugging at the cable but said nothing.

The girl looked down into the water. The lights lit the barrel like a Broadway star. "What are you *doing*?" she said again.

Lenny continued to ignore her questions. The hook finally connected with the lip of the barrel, and he pulled the cable taut. "Okay, reel it in," he said, his heart still sprinting in his throat.

"Fuck that," said the girl. "Tell me what you're doing."

Lenny looked at her but kept the tension on the cable with both hands. "I need to move it. Deeper."

The girl looked back into the water. "The barrel?"

Lenny nodded.

"What's in it?" she said, speaking slowly and narrowing her eyes.

"Just reel in the winch!" Lenny shouted at her.

"Fuck that!" she yelled back, her eyes widening. "There's a body in there! Just like the one they found on the beach!"

"No! No," said Lenny.

"It's not a body," said the girl, her tone skeptical. She folded her arms.

"No," said Lenny.

"Then what the hell is it?"

Lenny panicked. What is it, what is it, he thought. "Just some stuff."

"Some stuff," said the girl, now smiling, arms still folded. "Just some stuff."

"Yeah, some stuff," said Lenny. "It doesn't matter! I just need to move it!"

"Yeah it fuckin' matters," said the girl. "Like stolen stuff?" She grinned wider. "Pirate treasure?"

"Shut up!" said Lenny, still pulling on the cable. "Just run the winch, dammit!"

"This fishing trip just got a lot more expensive." She headed back to the console. Lenny noticed the bulge of the gun in her waistband. "Five hundred. Minimum," she said as she sat down in the driver's seat.

"You said two fifty!" Lenny's arms were getting tired.

"Five hundred or I'm out."

"I don't have it!"

"ATM in the store," she said, restarting the engines.

Lenny's hands ached from gripping the cable. Five hundred still seemed decent if it kept him out of prison. But five hundred? It was a lot of money. "Okay, okay, five hundred! I'll give it to you after!"

"This isn't gonna work. You need different equipment."

"Just run the winch," said Lenny.

She shook her head but flipped the switch, winding in the cable.

When it was tight, Lenny let go and shook out his hands. "Slowly," he said. The barrel tilted up, but once it stood on end, the hook slipped off. "Wait, it slipped."

"It's not gonna work," she said. "The hook won't grip the barrel."

"It has to work!" said Lenny, eyes wide, heart thumping.

"Needs a different attachment." She rested a fist against her lips while she thought. "One of those timber claws. For grabbing logs."

"You have one?" Lenny's eyes were like eggs.

"No," she said, "but I know where to get one. Tractor supply. In the city. Hundred bucks."

"They won't be open!" Lenny began to feel desperate.

"Not tonight, genius."

"When?" said Lenny.

"Tomorrow. It'll be another five-hundred, though. Special rate. For my special customer." She winked at him and made a clicking sound with her mouth. "And you buy the equipment."

7

THE GIRL GAVE LENNY an address in Boulder City, where he'd pick her up at noon the next day, and they'd head to the city for the timber claw. He didn't see the point in driving home, so he drank till closing at the Rusty Nail and slept in his truck, lit by the bar's neon sign. At eleven-thirty, he woke—head throbbing, neck kinked, cab already cooking in the late-morning sun—and called in sick. He drove through at a fast-food restaurant, dosed his coffee with Jack Daniel's, scarfed an egg and bacon sandwich, and arrived just before noon at the address—a sprawling Spanish ranch house with a manicured lawn and miniature palms.

Lenny's truck rattled to a stop, boat trailer still in tow, and the girl emerged from the house. As she started down the walkway toward the curb, a squat Asian woman, the same height as the girl, emerged onto the brick porch. "Grace!" she yelled.

The girl turned her head, but kept walking.

The woman waddled behind her, speaking loud and fast in a language foreign to Lenny. He got out of the truck and walked around to the curb. His head still hurt.

"The city!" the girl shouted over her shoulder.

The woman spoke again, this time louder, still pursuing the girl.

She arrived at the sidewalk and faced the woman, who'd stopped in the middle of the yard, shouting and gesturing toward Lenny's truck. "Mom!" The girl folded her arms and leaned back. "We're just getting fishing gear."

Her mother spoke another loud sentence in the foreign tongue.

The girl glanced up the street, sighed, and shook her head in disbelief. "I've got it," she said to her mother and patted the gun lodged in her waistband.

Her mom still seemed dissatisfied, but she turned and waddled back toward the house. She lobbed another sharp sentence, which made the girl chuckle. "She's crazy," she said to Lenny. "Let's go before she climbs in the back."

Lenny got in the truck, and the girl slid into the passenger's seat.

"Grace?" said Lenny, smiling.

She scowled at him and rolled down the window. "Your truck smells terrible."

Lenny blushed and checked his mirror. "What language was that?"

"Korean," said Grace.

As he rolled forward, Lenny looked out her window at the house once more. "Nice place," he said, admiring the facing tile under the porch steps. Shade from the trees gave the momentary illusion they didn't live in a desert hellscape. He pulled away from the curb without signaling and headed for the freeway. "Expensive. How'd they make their money?"

"Marina," said Grace. "Dad started it."

"So he didn't always drink."

Grace shook her head.

"Your mom knows about the gun?"

"She gave it to me."

"Gave it to you! Whoa," said Lenny. "How come?"

"Deal with creeps like you." Grace gave him a sideways look.

Lenny made a nervous laughing sound. "Okay, but seriously."

"Yeah. You talk too much," she said, then pointed to the road. "I'm not your buddy. We're moving a barrel."

Grace directed Lenny to the tractor supply store and picked out a bright red log grabber, a steel dragon claw with four spiky talons and a loop to clip to the winch cable. Lenny paid, and they got back in the truck. "I need to drop my boat at home."

"Then back to the marina," said Grace. "I gotta work."

When they arrived outside Lenny's trailer, Grace saw the paint peeling off the aluminum siding, the sagging porch, and the weeds growing through the rusty fence from his neighbor's side. "Nice place," she said, sarcasm oozing.

"Yeah, yeah," said Lenny.

After dropping off the boat, they drove to the exit of the trailer park. Traffic was jammed on Tropicana westbound, so Lenny waited for an opening, squeezed through, and turned east toward the Strip. Grace stared out the window at nothing. Lenny cut down to Hacienda, and suddenly she sprang to life. "Don't go this way," she said, her voice loud. "I don't go to the Strip."

Lenny looked at her, confused.

"Turn!" she shouted. "Don't go this way!"

"Relax! I'm just getting on the freeway," said Lenny.

"Turn!" She was screaming now.

Lenny turned. "Okay, okay," he said. "What the hell?"

"Just drive!" she shouted again.

Lenny found a different way to the freeway, avoiding the Strip. As they hooked onto the 215 toward Henderson, Grace stared out the side window. "You okay?" he asked. She turned on the radio, dialed to a country music station, and said nothing.

8

ENNY DROPPED GRACE AT the marina and drove
to a shaded lake overlook. He sat on his tailgate,
munching a hoagie, chasing with Jack Daniel's, pondering
Grace's episode. She seemed so hard with her gun, her
sketchy repair business, tough negotiations, punk style,
and her don't-give-a-shit attitude. But now a soft spot.

At seven, a little buzzed, Lenny parked at the marina,
took a last swig from a fresh pint bottle, and, after con-
firming the cops weren't around, walked up the dock ramp
with the timber claw. Outside the store, Grace's father
again sprawled in his chair, asleep, forty-ounce bottle empty. As before, his head tilted back, his mouth gaped, and
his snoring chopped the air like a saw. Grace emerged from
the store. As she locked the front door, she glanced at her
father, then looked at Lenny. "Cash," she said.

Lenny handed over five hundreds, again wondering who was getting the better deal.

They motored out to the spot. He moved to the bow and spied the barrel. Again the water looked shallower. Six feet now, he guessed. The sun had just set, and the lake glowed orange in the distance, as if its surface were on fire. "Need to wait a few minutes," he said. "Till it's dark."

"Cover of darkness," said Grace with a mocking tone.

Lenny shook his head and stared down at the metal barrel, its shape fading into the lake. "So why does your dad have this thing?" He slapped the side of the boat with his hand.

"He likes to fish," said Grace.

"Okay, but it's a serious offshore rig. Overkill on a lake, no?"

"When he bought it, he said he might take it to the ocean one day. He grew up fishing the ocean."

"California?"

"Korea," said Grace.

Lenny puckered his lips and nodded, impressed. "You born there?"

"No," she said. "Here. Henderson."

They waited another five minutes in silence. "Dark enough, Leonardo?" said Grace.

He rolled his eyes. "Dark enough."

Grace took the timber claw to the front of the boat and clipped it to the end of the cable, in place of the hook. She spread the talons to the diameter of a barrel and lowered the claw into the water. "Lights," she said.

Lenny returned to the console and hit the depth lights.

"Okay, drop it," she said. "Slowly."

Lenny let the winch out at half-speed while Grace metered the cable through her hands, guiding the claw toward the barrel.

"Bit more," said Grace. "Okay, hold up." She tugged and maneuvered the cable then gave it a jerk. "It's on. Reel it in. Slowly."

Lenny ran the winch, again at half-speed, sweating and praying under his breath.

After ten seconds or so, the claw surfaced, a spider crab pulled from the depths, and then the barrel. Lenny cut the winch motor, and the barrel gleamed in the floodlights, slowly rotating on the line. "Yes!" said Lenny, reflexively standing and pumping his fist.

From the console, he could see the claw's talons had punctured the rusty metal near the top of the barrel. As he opened his mouth to shout the next step, a sizable piece of the barrel and two talons broke free, the lid popped off, and the barrel tilted on its side. A waxy, white substance slipped out, along with pieces that looked like bones, followed by a cracked skull. A powerful smell of ammonia washed over the boat. Lenny watched, horrified, as the skull and bones disappeared below, along with the denser-looking pieces. Other white chunks bobbed at the surface. "No!" Lenny gaped at the water and then slumped into the driver's seat, beginning to hyperventilate.

Grace gagged. "What the fuck was that!"

Seconds later, another boat approached at speed, bathing them in its floodlights.

"Cut the depth lights and drop the claw!" said Grace.

Lenny did as she said. Seconds later, the other boat was on them, the silver and orange vessel from the night before. Over a bullhorn, Lenny heard, "Coast Guard. Remain where you are." He continued to hyperventilate.

The Coast Guard vessel drew alongside them, floodlights still trained on their boat. Two men were on board, one in the cabin, at the helm, and the other, seemingly the captain, on the narrow deck outside the cabin door. The captain addressed Grace, no longer with the bullhorn, shouting over the sound of idling engines: "Where are your navigation lights?"

"We're anchored," Grace shouted back.

The captain waved his hand, and his mate cut the engines. "Still need them on at night," said the captain, his voice stern. Then, in a more familiar tone, "Grace?"

"Parker," said Grace, eyeing the waxy pieces still floating off the bow.

"What are you all doing out here?"

"We were planning to fish."

"How many on board?"

"Just the two of us," said Grace, nodding toward Lenny.

The captain eyed Lenny, who was still breathing too fast, face in his hands. "He okay?"

"Yeah. Seasick," said Grace.

"Where are you heading?"

"Now? Back to the marina," said Grace.

"Any weapons on board?"

"No," said Grace without hesitation.

"I'm going to board for a quick inspection," said the captain. He looped a line around a cleat on their boat and stepped across.

Lenny sat up and took a slow, shaky breath.

"I need to see your safety card and registration," said the captain. "Also, the passenger list."

"Oh, he's a friend, not a client," said Grace. "So no list." She walked to the console, reached into a compartment across from the passenger seat, and produced the other documents. While at the console, she flicked on the navigation lights. The captain examined the documents with a flashlight and then handed them back. He walked to the stern to examine the engines and anchor. "Life jackets?"

"Under the seat, there," said Grace.

He checked the life jackets. "Flares and fire extinguisher?"

"In the front." Grace walked back to the bow, and the captain followed. She opened a compartment, drawing out two flares and a fire extinguisher.

The captain examined them, passed them back, and paused. "What's on the line?" he said, pointing to the winch cable that disappeared into the water.

"Another anchor," said Grace. "He needs two." She flashed a wry smile and nodded toward Lenny.

The captain didn't smile. He looked into the water, but the angle of his floodlights allowed only a foot or two of visibility. "What's all that white stuff?" he said, pointing to the waxy pieces still floating near the winch cable.

Grace glanced over the bow. She raised her eyebrows and frowned, looking confused. "Dunno. Styrofoam?"

"Doesn't look like styrofoam," he said. "Looks like wax."

Grace shrugged. "Weird."

The captain turned back to the boat, looked around for a few more seconds, then pulled out a pad and began scribbling. He tore off a page and handed it to Grace. "Report of Boarding. Everything looks okay. Just keep it for records."

Grace nodded and tucked the paper in the compartment with the other documents. "Anything else?" she said.

"No, that's it." The captain unhooked the line and stepped across to his boat. "Have a safe night," he said. "And get your friend to shore." He waved to his partner, who fired up their engines, and the vessel sped away, out onto the lake.

Grace pulled the gun from her waistband and pointed at Lenny, whose eyes widened. "A body? A fuckin' body?" said Grace, yelling at him. "You said it wasn't a body! Are you fuckin' kidding me?"

Lenny instinctively stood and put his hands in the air. His heart thrashed in his chest.

"Did you do it?"

"Do what?" said Lenny.

"Come on! Did you kill the guy?"

Lenny froze, his mind fogged, unable to respond.

"Okay. I see." She racked the slide on her pistol, sending a round into the chamber.

"No! It wasn't me!"

"Bullshit!" said Grace. She adjusted her grip on the gun.

"Okay, okay!" Lenny shouted, looking down at the dashboard to avoid seeing the gun. His whole body shook. "It was forty years ago."

Grace blinked back tears. "Once a murderer, always a fucking murderer!"

Lenny winced.

She held the gun steady. "Why'd you kill him?" Lenny didn't respond. "Why'd you kill him!?" She shouted at him.

He wiped his nose on his sleeve and cleared his throat twice. "My boss told me to."

"Your boss told you to."

"You didn't say 'no' to him," said Lenny.

"Who the hell was your boss?" Grace still trained her pistol on him.

"Tony Bonucci," said Lenny.

Grace blinked. "Like . . . the guy in the mob museum? *Tony Bonucci* Tony Bonucci?"

Lenny nodded.

"You *are* a fuckin' mobster. I knew it! Damn!" Grace lowered her gun in amazement and then jerked it back to eye level.

"Used to be," said Lenny. "Barely."

Grace looked skeptical. "That other body," she said, nodding toward shore. "Hemenway Harbor Doe. That one yours too?"

"No. My partner's." Lenny's shoulders felt tired from lifting his arms. He wiped his nose with his hand. "Can you put the gun away now?"

Grace scoffed, still aiming at him. "Who was this guy?" She gestured toward the winch cable with the gun.

"A hotel valet. Used to tip Tony off about rich guests. So he could rob them. Cops flipped him. He was gonna testify."

"So you killed him," said Grace. She grit her teeth and tears welled in her eyes again.

"Tony would've killed me if I didn't."

Grace looked unimpressed.

"I was young! It was my only hit!" Lenny started shaking again.

"Okay, okay," said Grace, blinking back tears. She sighed. "You shouldn't have lied." She tucked the gun back in her waistband.

"So you could blab to the cops?" said Lenny. He slumped into the passenger's seat, exhausted.

Grace moved to the console and slipped into the driver's seat beside him. "You don't blab, I don't blab," she said.

Lenny glanced at her. "I'm still screwed." His voice was deflated. "It's in a hundred pieces. We'll never move it now. The lake drops another six feet and it'll be on the beach."

"Maybe the fish will eat it," said Grace.

"Not the bones," said Lenny. "They just found a skeleton in Callville Bay. Been there for years."

"Well, so what if they find it?" said Grace. "How will they know it's yours?"

"Human remains scattered beside broken barrel pieces? First person they'll talk to is my old partner."

"He's still around?" said Grace.

Lenny nodded and sighed. "I heard he gives tours of old mobster sites in the city. Cops probably already talked to him about the first barrel."

"He can't talk or he goes down with you."

"Well, that's just it. He can say whatever he wants. He's immune. He turned informant. Did two years in the joint and two more in Witness Protection. The whole thing. They can't touch him. One word from him and I'm done."

"Well, if he was an informant, wouldn't he have told the cops about the bodies already?"

"Apparently not these two. Paper said the FBI was investigating the first one. And if they knew about mine, they'd have hauled it up already."

Grace thought a moment. "Think he'll talk?"

"I don't know," said Lenny. "He didn't forty years ago. But I hear he found religion. Probably all into telling the truth and shit."

"Well, he doesn't have to tell everything," said Grace. "He live in the city?"

Lenny nodded.

"You need to get to him first. Convince him not to talk."

"That sounds real fuckin' easy," said Lenny.

Grace paused. "What kind of religion?"

"I don't know," said Lenny. "He's Chicago Italian. Catholic?"

"Mmm. Christian. My parents are Christian. Well, my mom is. Dad used to be. I know all about that shit. They used to drag me to church every week." She paused again. "Could go either way. Depends whether he's a lover or a hater. The love-Christians are all about forgiveness. But the haters just want punishment."

Grace unlocked the door, and they stepped into the store. Over the hum of the drink coolers, Lenny heard what sounded like hurt-animal noises coming from the back. "What's that?"

Grace placed her index finger across her mouth and whispered, "Stay here." She headed down the middle aisle and nudged open a door in the back wall. In the low light,

Lenny could see Grace's father, sitting on the floor, against a desk, rocking and keening, his face streaked with tears. "Dad," said Grace, her voice a mix of embarrassment and compassion. She crouched down and put her arms around him. He began to sob quietly. "It's okay," she said. "You're okay." She held him for a while. He stopped crying and stared at the floor.

Grace stood up again, retrieved a laptop from the desk, stepped through the doorway, and pulled the door mostly closed. She dropped into the chair behind the cash register.

"Everything okay?" said Lenny

Her face showed no emotion. She had the laptop open. "When does your partner run his tours?"

"He's not my partner. And no idea," said Lenny, still thinking about Grace's father.

She moved her finger over the trackpad and clicked at the keyboard. "Frank Messina?"

Lenny nodded.

"Looks like they run every day but Sunday, ten and two o'clock. Start at the Peppermill."

"Figures," said Lenny. "Tony's guys used to love that place." Tony had once bought Lenny breakfast there, when he first started working for him. It was one of the few places on the Strip that hadn't changed much since those days.

"Tour tomorrow?" said Grace.

"Gotta work," said Lenny.

"When's your next day off?"

"Saturday. But I'm not sure this is a good idea."

"It's the only idea," said Grace.

"You're coming?"

"Someone's gotta stop you fuckin' it up."

Lenny smiled. "You know it's on the Strip."

"That part's okay," said Grace. "Pick me up Saturday at nine."

9

THE NEXT DAY, AS Lenny drove his bulldozer, he fretted over what to do. He imagined Frank as a bitter old man. He'd done Tony's dirty work for years, and when he finally got caught, Tony ordered a hit on *him*. Because Frank informed on the Outfit, he got a shortened sentence, but he still did time, and when he came out, he'd have been the Outfit's prime target. Lenny imagined his fugitive life in Witness Protection, shifting from state to state, staying off the radar, at least till the nineties when the casinos went corporate and memories had faded.

The Outfit wouldn't worry Frank anymore—they'd whacked Tony themselves, and the FBI had long since confined them to Chicago. Frank had found a way to cash in on his ugly past. But what did he *think* about that past? Were the tours just a way to make money? Just one more

Vegas spectacle, a macabre brand of theater at home on the modern Strip? Or were they a way to cling to his past? Did Frank still think of himself as a mobster, deep down? In either case, it seemed there was a chance Frank wouldn't give Lenny up.

What about Frank's religion? Maybe it was just part of the show, duping the cops into thinking he'd "gone straight." But what if it was sincere? Were the tours a kind of confession, airing the truth of what he once was as a path to healing? Public atonement for damage done? As he'd told Grace, if the religion were sincere, Frank might feel compelled to spill it all, regardless of consequences. Frank was such a hard-ass, a visit from Lenny might only *deepen* his commitment to talk. Frank had paid the price, so why would he just let Lenny off?

But, of course, Frank likely wouldn't talk unless the valet's body turned up. And it was still possible the scattered bones, waxy flesh, and pieces of corroded barrel would stay underwater. Maybe the lake had reached its low point. What if there was rain and snow in the future and the lake refilled? If so, thought Lenny, he might find religion himself.

After work, Lenny went to the library and looked up Lake Mead levels on a computer. It'd dropped six inches each day for the past ten days.

On Friday, the heat was punishing. The sun scorched Lenny's forearms angry pink through the tinted glass of the dozer cab. He returned to the library after work: the lake had continued to drop. The Thursday measurement showed another six-inch decline from the day before. If the barrel had been in eight feet of water last Saturday, he estimated the remains of the valet were now only five feet deep. By tomorrow, the valet's skull could be shallow enough for someone to step on while swimming.

Lenny and Grace pulled into the parking lot of the Peppermill at nine forty-five. They backed into a spot near the edge so they could see the entire lot. The rainbow neon sign was new, but the flat top and swooping curve of the roof were familiar, like the restaurant wore a huge fedora made of asphalt shingles. Lenny turned on the radio. A reporter was telling a story about the crisis on the Colorado River. He turned it off again. He gripped, ungripped, and regripped the steering wheel.

"Stop it!" said Grace. "You're making me nervous."

Five minutes later, a white transit van with dark windows pulled into the parking lot, and two people stepped out of the restaurant, one a man-mountain, at least as tall as Lenny, thick with muscles, and the other, beyond a doubt, his old partner, Frank. Though he wore a hat and showed more barrel than chest, the bowed legs, snake-skin derbies (same old pair?), slacks, untucked shirt, and thick tinted glasses were unmistakably Frank. The two men waited beside the van, and a small crowd began to gather. Frank smoked a cigarette.

Lenny and Grace got out of the truck and walked across the parking lot. The man-mountain eyed them, unfolding his arms as they approached. Lenny's fresh shirt was already soaked in the armpits. "Frank," said Lenny, over the buzz of the growing crowd.

Frank looked at him, puzzled.

"Lenny Battaglia."

Recognition dawned, his eyebrows arched, and Frank said, too slowly, "Lenny Battaglia." Frank reached out his right hand, and Lenny shook it. "Wondered when you might turn up."

"Long time," said Lenny.

Frank shook his head in amazement, puffed out his cheeks, released them, and chuckled. "You got that right." Then he furrowed his brow into a question mark. "You're not here for the tour."

"No," said Lenny. "I need to talk."

Frank looked at him. "Sounds serious."

Lenny didn't deny it.

"Well," said Frank, "I can't talk now." He gestured toward the transit van. "Lunch at noon?" Frank pointed over his shoulder with his thumb, toward the entrance to the Peppermill.

Lenny nodded. "See you at noon."

CHAPTER 9 ¾

AFTER WORK, LENNY WENT straight to the Spring Valley Library, a short drive from the trailer park. He crossed the lobby and arrowed toward the reference desk. A matronly librarian sat behind the desk on a padded rolling chair. Bifocals inset with faux diamonds rested on her full cheeks and magnified her judgmental eyes. Her permed hair was an unnatural shade of red, and Lenny spotted gray in the part. Her name tag said "Phyllis Turnbull." She reminded him vaguely of his ex-wife. He was suddenly aware he hadn't changed his clothes since leaving the dump.

"Hi Phyllis," said Lenny.

She stared back at him.

"I need some help." Weren't librarians supposed to be friendly? "How do I find information on the level of Lake Mead?"

She rolled the chair in front of her computer and started typing on the keyboard.

Had she ignored him? "Hello?"

"I'm looking," she said, her tone condescending. After more typing and a few clicks of her mouse, she scribbled something on a scrap of paper, slid it across the countertop toward Lenny, and rolled back to the computer.

Lenny looked at the paper. She'd written a long chain of characters with no spaces. He made out the words "lake" and "mead," but, apart from those, her writing was gibberish. "What's this?"

She looked up from the computer screen and raised a thinly-painted eyebrow. "Really?"

Lenny blinked twice, feeling stupid.

"It's a url," she said. "A web address?"

He smiled nervously and shook his head.

"Like, for a computer," she said.

"Oh," said Lenny. "I don't know about that."

The librarian stared at him, incredulous. "You live under a rock?"

Lenny blushed. "No, I..."

She sighed, got up from her chair, walked out from behind the desk, and started across the library floor. "Follow me," she said without looking over her shoulder.

Lenny clutched the paper with the computer words and shuffled after her. He felt glad to be divorced.

The librarian led him to a long table separated into six carrels, each with a bulky computer monitor, keyboard, and mouse. "Sit," she said, directing him to the swivel stool in front of the monitor. "Click here," she said, leaning toward the screen and pointing with her finger. Lenny caught a whiff of cheap perfume. She waited for him to figure out the mouse. He finally clicked. "Now type that," she said, pointing to the paper.

"All of it?"

"Yes," she said, exasperated. "All of it."

Lenny looked back and forth between the paper and the computer screen, pecking out the letters and numbers with his right index finger. He heard a sigh from behind him, and when he turned, the librarian was already halfway to the reference desk.

A few minutes later, Lenny finished entering the strange character string. He looked up and waved at the librarian.

Without looking at him, she raised her hand, index finger extended, suggesting she'd be there in a minute.

When she returned to the carrel, Lenny said, "I typed it," and pointed to his work.

"Hit Enter," she said.

Lenny hit the Enter key, and the screen changed to a table of little numbers. The lefthand column had dates, and the fourth column had the heading "Lake Mead Elevation." Numbers were filled in for each day up to the present. The spaces for the rest of the month were blank. Finally something made sense, thought Lenny. "Okay, got it," he said, staring at the screen. The librarian went back to her desk.

Lenny squinted at the numbers. The lake had dropped around six inches each day for the past week and a half. He stared at the blank spaces under the elevation numbers, as if the future measurements were merely hidden behind the white pixels and, with the right password, he'd be able to see them.

He plucked a blunt pencil from a mesh cup beside the monitor and scribbled the word "enter" under the string of characters the librarian had given him. He got up, slipped the paper into his pocket, and made for the exit.

10

T HEY GOT BACK IN the truck. "Thanks for the introduction," said Grace.

Lenny ignored her comment, his face grim. He started the engine and cranked the air conditioner. Rattling and pinging issued from the vents, along with air, only marginally cooler than outside.

"Your AC is shit," said Grace.

Lenny stared out the windshield at the tour van, entranced.

"So what now?" said Grace, shoving him to get his attention.

Lenny looked at her, still dazed, and blinked. "I don't know," he said.

"Well, I'm not sitting in this truck for two hours waiting for mister mobster to finish his tour."

Lenny continued to look at Grace. He was glad she'd come with him. He smiled at her. "Go for a drive down the Strip?"

"Fuck you," she said, chuckling.

"How's your dad?"

"He's all right," said Grace. "Well . . . not really."

"What's up with all that?"

Grace looked Lenny in the eye. "You really wanna know?"

Lenny looked back at her, considering, then said, "Yeah. I do."

"Okay," she said. "Drive."

Grace directed Lenny to a parking lot behind a sex shop. "What's this?" said Lenny, eyeing the sign over the entrance that read, Where the Fun Begins, in lipstick-pink cursive.

"Not that!" said Grace. "Just park, you pervert."

When they got out of the truck, Grace led Lenny a half-block down the street to what looked like a small park. At the entrance, both sides of a large black double gate stood open, and on the arch overhead were the words, "Healing Garden." Grace entered and started along a walkway encircling a large heart-shaped planter. Lenny followed, enjoying the shade of the leafy trees. Four-foot green metal frames like trellises stood beside the walkway, anchored in the ground, each with a plate or sign bearing a person's name. Countless mementos covered the frames, as if the garden grew memories instead of plants: flags, photos, ribbons, stars, words, flowers, angels, hearts, and rocks on the ground with painted letters spelling "Vegas Strong." Grace sat on the edge of the planter and patted the spot next to her. Lenny sat down.

"Know why we're here?" she said.

Lenny shook his head.

Grace pointed across the path to a frame with the name, "Kwan Kim."

Lenny looked at the name plate. "Family?"

"My brother. It'll be five years in October."

Lenny gave a solemn nod. He remembered the events of five years ago. In the span of ten minutes, a gunman had fired over a thousand rounds from a hotel window into the crowd at a country music festival. Sixty-one people dead, including the shooter. "I've heard about this place," said Lenny.

"He was working security at the festival," said Grace. "He'd just started at UNLV. Got me a free ticket."

"You were there?"

"I got out when the shooting started, but he didn't make it. His coworker said he was keeping people from trampling each other. Took a bullet to the head." Grace stared at the ground. "He didn't need the job. He had a big scholarship, and my parents could have written a check for the rest. They made him work. 'Builds character,' they said." Tears welled in her eyes. "Fuck character." She wiped her eyes with the butt of her hand and snorted to stop her nose from dripping. "That's why I avoid the Strip. Or at least that part. And why Dad cries."

Lenny said nothing.

"Shooter was the son of a criminal," said Grace. "Gambler. Divorced. No kids. Alcoholic. Cops still don't know why he did it."

Lenny leaned forward and looked at the paving stones between his feet. "Suppose its forty years later," he said. "And the cops never caught the guy. If you met him. D'you turn him in?"

Grace looked at him. "This ain't about you, man. But hell yeah, I'd turn him in."

Lenny blushed and felt nauseous.

11

Lenny and Grace stepped inside the Peppermill
just before noon. Semi-circular booths lined with
royal blue, aqua, and purple velour clustered around fake
cherry trees in full bloom. Frank hadn't arrived, so they
watched the parking lot through tinted windows. Lenny
rubbed his hands on his slacks, trying to dry off the sweat.

The tour van pulled in, emptying near the restaurant
entrance. Enthused tourists snapped selfies with Frank
and his heavy. Lenny and Grace went outside when the
crowd had thinned, Lenny's heartbeat thumping in his
ears.

"One thing," said Frank, after introductions. "I don't
do guns."

"May I?" said Lewis, Frank's heavy, already patting
Lenny down.

As Lewis turned to pat down Grace, she put her hand up and said, "Whoa, whoa, whoa."

"Concealed carry?" said Frank.

"It's not for you, Frank. She always has it."

"I always have it," said Grace.

"Well, it stays out here or we don't talk. I don't do guns."

"One minute," said Lenny and drew Grace aside.

"What the fuck," hissed Grace. "I'm not ditching my gun." Her eyes drilled into Lenny.

"I'm sorry, I didn't know," said Lenny, quietly. "Wait in the truck?"

"No fuckin' . . ." said Grace, too loudly, and then clarified with a whisper, "No fuckin' way. Your AC sucks, it's a hundred degrees, and I need lunch."

Lenny looked at the pavement, then up at Grace. "So talk to Frank another time? Lunch somewhere else?"

Grace looked over at Frank and Lewis. "Shit," she said. "I'll leave it in the truck. But you *owe* me."

Lenny felt relieved. "Thanks," he whispered. He looked over at Frank. "We're gonna put it in the truck. Just give us a second."

"We'll get a table," said Frank, looking cheerful.

Lenny put the gun in the glove box, and he and Grace returned to the restaurant. After escorting them to Frank's booth, the hostess handed them enormous menus.

"Lunch on me," said Frank.

Lenny looked up, his eyes fighting for focus. "Very generous," he said, trying to sound calm, studying the menu in silence.

Frank looked at him. "So how you been?"

"Good," said Lenny. He felt Frank trying to read his mind.

"Still at the dump?"

Lenny nodded.

"That's a long time. Close to retirement?"

"Yep."

"Tony really set you up there."

"I guess you could say that," said Lenny. After the hit, Tony had dropped the compassionate father act and became the angry boss. He sat Lenny on his faux-leather couch, pacing in front of him. *Girl. Baby. Whiner.* Those are the words Lenny remembered. And the sting of Tony's backhand on his face. "Out?" he said. "Out?" Another backhand. "You don't get out. Nobody gets out. Only guy gets out is the guy at the bottom of the lake." Still, Tony could see that Lenny wasn't cut out for the work. The dump was union-controlled, and the Outfit controlled the union. Pushing trash was just a way for Tony to keep an eye on him, make sure he didn't go talking.

The waitress took their orders. Grace got a club sandwich, Lenny a cheeseburger, Lewis got salmon, and Frank ordered a porterhouse with a Bloody Mary. "Tequila Sunrise," said Grace after hearing Frank's drink order.

Frank looked at Grace and chuckled. "So why's a nice young lady like yourself carry a gun?"

Grace smiled, eyes locked on Frank. "Why's a thug like Lewis carry one?"

Frank laughed with the deep-lung wheeze of a lifetime smoker and then fell into a coughing fit. When he regained control, he looked back at Grace, nodding and smiling. "I like you." He turned to Lenny. "Your girlfriend's funny!"

"Not his girlfriend," said Grace. "I like women."

Frank ignored her comment and took a sip of water. "So what's on your mind, Lenny?"

Lenny felt the blood drain from his face. The waitress brought the drinks. Grace gulped at her cocktail. Lenny gave her a side-eye and wished he'd ordered some alcohol:

it'd seemed too early for public whiskey. "I, ah . . . well . . . you been reading the papers?"

"Yeah, what about 'em?"

"Hemenway Harbor Doe?"

"Okay, yeah," said Frank. "I thought that might be it." He paused. "Not a Doe any more. I talked to the feds the day after the barrel showed up."

Lenny's heart sped. "What'd you tell them."

"Ah, you know. Who the guy was. Whether I was involved, the normal stuff."

Lenny looked over his shoulder, leaned toward Frank, and used a quieter voice: "You tell 'em you killed the guy?"

Frank nodded. "I got nothin' to hide. The cops know I was a bad guy. I did my time. Can't touch me now."

Lenny nodded, heart still hammering inside him. "You mention me?"

Frank read Lenny's face. "Nah," he said. "They didn't want all the details. I told 'em Tony ordered the hit. They don't care who helped me dump the barrel." Frank took a sip from his drink. "All that's ancient history."

Lenny realized he hadn't been breathing. He sighed and sat back in his seat. It seemed Frank wasn't inclined to blab about Lenny's role in the murders.

Grace stared at Frank. "What about the other barrel?" She chewed the maraschino cherry from her drink, stem poking through her lips.

Frank looked at her, then at Lenny. "She knows a lot."

Lenny raised his eyebrows. "Yes, she does."

"Well," said Frank, then sipped his Bloody Mary. "It hasn't showed up yet. And I'm not in the habit of telling cops what they don't ask about."

"What if it shows up?" said Grace. "And they ask about it."

Lenny felt as if a clamp were tightening around his head.

"Depends what they ask," said Frank. He sipped his drink.

The waitress and a busboy arrived with the food. They set down the plates, and the waitress said, "Can I get y'all anything else?"

"No thanks, doll," said Frank, clutching her butt and squeezing. "Looks delicious."

The waitress giggled. Grace fumed.

After ten eternal seconds, they left the table, and Lenny leaned in again. "Would you tell them about me?"

Frank sliced into his rare steak; bloody juice spread over his plate. "Well, if they ask who killed him . . ." He let the implication dangle. The table fell silent as Frank chewed his bite.

The waitress returned. "How is everything?"

"Fantastic," said Frank and winked at her.

The waitress left.

Grace furrowed her brow and looked at Lenny, who stared into his lap, cheeseburger untouched. She turned to Frank. "If they ask who killed him, you *lie*."

Frank chuckled and looked at Lenny. "Firecracker!" He took another bite of steak and chewed with his mouth open. "Honey, I'm a man of God. I can't be lying. 'Thou shalt not tell a lie.'"

"Bullshit," said Grace. "The commandment says, 'You shall not bear false witness against your neighbor.' You wouldn't be harming any neighbors. You'd be helping one. Plenty of Bible people lied."

Frank swallowed his bite and looked at Lenny. "What is she, your lawyer?"

Lenny continued staring into his lap, heart pounding. He felt paralyzed.

"What's that Bible lady's name?" said Grace. "The one who hid the Jewish spies and lied about it? Rahab. Yeah, Rahab. She was doing the right thing."

"Maybe she was," said Frank. "I don't know about her. But what I do know is if I lie to the cops, and they find out, I go back to prison. That's my deal."

"How are they gonna find out?" said Grace. "Just tell 'em you did it."

"Look," said Frank, irritated. "I'm not gonna lie, okay, so you can drop it, sweetie."

"I'm not your sweetie," said Grace and took an angry bite of her sandwich.

"Lenny," said Frank, chewing another bite of steak.

Lenny looked up, his face white like sun-bleached bones.

"You're worried about the wrong things. The cops. The body. They're eating away at you."

Lenny felt Frank's eyes burrowing into him.

"You gotta bring all this into the light. Stuff rots in the dark," said Frank. "Look at me. It's all out there. Nothin' to hide." Frank spread his arms, palms open. "Light as a feather. Confession. Makes you free."

Easy for Frank to say, thought Lenny, roused by annoyance. He doesn't go to prison if he tells the truth. Sure, he did his time, but it's not like his confession was some selfless act; Tony had a hit out on him. His choice was either talk to the cops and get a reduced sentence, or deal with Tony's hitman and face a longer sentence—if he survived. Lenny's choice was completely different: hide and maybe stay out of prison, or confess and die there. The cops wouldn't be offering *him* a plea deal. Tony was dead, so there was no one left to rat on. "You're free 'cause someone else paid your debt," said Lenny.

"Exactly," said Frank, "And his name is Jesus."

Lenny's face flashed hot. He'd heard enough. "His name was Tony fuckin' Bonucci. He's six feet underground. Where's your honor?"

"Honor? You're talking about honor? We killed people, Lenny. We robbed and pillaged and did terrible things. Get a load of you. Honor. You think you're better than me? At least I did the job I was given."

"Until you ratted out your boss."

"And what about you? One hit and you were begging to get out. Cryin' in your Cheerios."

"Cause I knew it was wrong."

"Then be done with it! Turn yourself in! Or put a bullet in your brain! Don't come to me with your little girlfriend asking me to lie for you. You with all your honor." Frank leaned back against the booth cushioning. "Tony ruined you, Lenny. Like he ruined us all."

Lenny boiled inside, but he had no reply. He hated to admit it, but Frank was right: there was no honor in what they'd done. Lenny stood, wiped his mouth with his napkin, and tossed it on the table. He gestured toward Grace. "Whatever happens, just leave her out of it."

Frank stared at Lenny and finally nodded.

"Thanks for lunch." Lenny headed for the door, his burger untouched.

Grace gulped down the last of her drink, scrambled to her feet, and issued a parting shot: "Bet your tour is shit."

12

F OR THE NEXT FIVE days, Lenny drove the dozer with a whisky buzz and checked lake levels after work at the library. They continued to drop. By Thursday, he figured the body and barrel were in no more than two feet of water.

When he got home that evening, he filled a tall water glass with Jack Daniel's, as if it were beer, dropped in an ice cube, and settled into the worn recliner, paying no attention to the gameshow on television. He took a long first drink and then sipped, ice jingling against the glass in his jittery hand. It felt like the hot walls of his trailer were pressing in.

It couldn't be more than a couple of days before someone noticed the broken barrel and bones on the shoreline. A day after that and the cops would talk to Frank. Should he get in his truck and drive? Where would he go? California? Arizona? Get lost in the desert? Might buy a couple of months, but sooner or later they'd find him. He couldn't keep running. Mexico? What kind of life would that be? Wherever he went, he wouldn't outrun the conflagration of guilt that roiled and swirled inside him, tamped for a time by whiskey but never extinguished.

One thing he felt sure of: he wouldn't go to prison. He thought of his dad, stuck in the Victorville Pen for ten years, and then, with little explanation, dead. "Accidental causes" was the official word. Gang violence? Infection? Whatever the euphemism hid, it wasn't pleasant. Lenny was still so big he'd draw attention from the alphas in the yard, and he felt too old to punch his way through. He just couldn't muster the anger anymore. Living out his days in a cinderblock cell, eating prison food, shitting in front of his cellmate, with no hope of release? He'd rather die.

The phone rang, startling Lenny from his dark rumination. It hadn't rung in months. Who could possibly have his number? He set his drink down and stood with a grunt. He picked up the phone after the third ring.

"You're hard to get ahold of," said Grace.

"That's the idea," said Lenny.

"You still got my gun." He'd seen it there in the glove box all week as he imbibed in the parking lot before work. "I need it back," she said.

"Okay, yeah," said Lenny. "I'll bring it after work tomorrow night."

Despite three tall whiskeys, Lenny barely slept. All night he tangled and sweat in his sheets, and he thought of his mother. She'd swallowed her pills in a back bedroom like his. He'd always resented her for it, leaving him alone. The Bonuccis had filled the void, and, until a few days ago, Lenny had thought of Tony as his savior, his deliverer. But Frank was right: Tony had ruined him, twisting his life into knots he couldn't untie. Tony's help wasn't selfless; he'd wanted Lenny's fists. It seemed to him now that Tony had used his vulnerability, grooming him for evil.

Had his mother's act been cowardly? For years, he'd thought so. But now he wasn't so sure. He got how tired she must have felt. Years of struggle stretching in front of her, and no way to get a foothold, no way to breathe.

Lenny drank and drove his way through the next day, imagining the wrecked barrel in the shallow water he hoped still covered the valet's bones.

After work, he changed clothes at home and sweat through the armpits of his fresh shirt as he connected the boat trailer to his truck. He rattled into the bank parking lot just before closing and withdrew his remaining $10,326. "Yes," said Lenny when the teller asked if he wanted to close the account.

The sun had set when he arrived at the marina. Two empty bottles stood outside the store, but Grace's father wasn't there, and the door was locked. Back in 10 Minutes. Lenny chuckled at the sign and realized he felt calm.

He licked the seal on the envelope with the money, pressing the sticky flap closed, and wrote "Grace" on the back. He thought for a second and added, "Sorry about the gun." He pushed the envelope through the store's mail slot.

Lenny rumbled down the mile-long boat ramp. The moon had risen, and the smell of warm desert sand drifted in the window. The once-floating dock now rested on mud. The silver water shimmered in the distance, across the flats.

He backed the truck and trailer to the ramp's end, beside the dock, and stopped. He took a deep breath, exhaled slowly, grabbed the passenger headrest with his right arm so he could twist around and look out the back window, and gunned it, trying to keep the boat straight. The rig launched onto the flat, traveling twenty yards before the rear wheels began to spin. Another five yards and the wheels dug holes, halting the truck and trailer in a spray of mud.

Lenny killed the engine. He opened the glove box, pulled out the flashlight and Grace's gun, and reached back for the pint bottle of whiskey. He drained it in three gulps, grimaced, and tucked the gun into his waistband. After clipping the flashlight to his belt, he walked back to the trailer, mud sucking at his shoes with each step. He lowered the boat and began dragging it the remaining fifty yards to the water.

As he neared the shoreline, his shoes sank deeper in the mud, each step more laborious than the last. At the shore, his foot stuck, and he freed it only by slipping out of the leather shoe, now entombed in mud. He watched water fill the shoe and felt a surge of anger. He ripped off his sock, leaned heavily on his bare foot, and wrenched his still-shod foot from the muck. He pulled off the remaining shoe and sock, flinging them into the water ahead of him.

He scanned the shoreline, expecting the carcass of the metal barrel, jagged pieces piercing the water. Where was it? He dragged the boat along the shore, sweeping the flashlight across the shallows. He caught sight of a bone just below the surface. A femur? Then another—maybe a pelvis. But no broken barrel, no metal pieces. Adrenaline surged. If there was no barrel, then the bones could just be a drowning victim, like the one they'd found last week at Callville Bay. Even if the cops consulted Frank about the bones, without the barrel there was no clear tie to Lenny. His insides leapt.

Then he saw the cracked skull, a foot below on the lake bed, glowing white in the flashlight beam, and he remembered the man's face as he cowered on the concrete floor of the garage. A face he'd destroyed. A human face. The empty eye sockets stared up at him, dark, pleading.

He waded to where the water was deep enough to use the engine and clambered into the boat. He flipped the outboard over the transom, into the water. Through tear-blurred vision, he adjusted the trim on the Evinrude and pulled the cord. The engine started on the first try, and he thought of Grace. A hundred bucks for a stolen fuel pump. She was sneaky. And funny. And kind. Her gun dug into the small of his back. Could he do this? Would she care? He looked over at the marina, its yellow-green lights smeared on the lake. Revving the motor, he steered away from shore.

Lenny cut the engine and drifted into the slip next to the Kims' white boat. He tied off the painter, climbed out, and started down the dock to the store.

"Lenny!"

He turned and saw Grace emerging from her clandestine workshop. "I was looking for you," he said.

"You got my gun?" she said, and then looked at his bare feet. "Why are you muddy? Where's your shoes?"

Lenny handed her the gun. "I need a phone."

"My cell," said Grace, handing it to him. "What's going on?"

Lenny ignored her and tapped the phone with his finger. He held it to his face. "Las Vegas Boat Harbor," he said, after a few seconds. "The marina store."

Grace looked at Lenny and narrowed her eyes. "What are you doing?"

"Police," said Lenny, into the phone.

"Lenny, what are you doing?" Grace raised her voice. "Don't do that!"

Lenny waved his hand to quiet her.

"I already moved the barrel!" said Grace, almost shouting.

"What's the emergency?" said the operator into Lenny's ear.

He paused and looked at Grace.

She looked back at him, her eyes now wide.

Lenny held the phone steady against his face. "I killed a man."

THE END

Acknowledgements

This novella was based on actual events of 2022, namely the decline of Lake Mead to its lowest level since first filling in 1941, and the discovery of a body in a barrel on the lake's shore. The body was dressed in clothing from the late 1970s or early 80s and exhibited a gunshot wound, both of which suggested to authorities that the killing was a mob hit. As of the time of publication, the victim has not yet been identified, though investigations are ongoing. Based on the evidence, there are three main candidates, outlined in a 2022 article.[1] In my story, the victim is not based on any of these leading candidates, though I did imagine him as swept up in the real-world practice of using private information to rob wealthy hotel-casino guests.

The perpetrator of the hit also remains unknown, but the era and style of the killing makes Tony Spilotro, the Chicago Outfit's enforcer in Las Vegas at that time, the most likely mastermind. My character, Tony Bonucci, is loosely based on Spilotro, and my Frank Messina is loosely based on Frank Cullotta, the one-time leader of Spilotro's "Hole in the Wall Gang," who robbed Las Vegas businesses by punching holes in walls to avoid detection by security systems.

Lenny Battaglia is wholly a product of my imagination, though the murder he committed was based on the actual murder of Jerry Lisner, ordered by Spilotro and carried out by Cullotta in 1979. Grace Kim was also my invention, though the tragedy that struck her family was, of course, based on the actual 2017 mass shooting in which Stephen Paddock fired over 1,000 rounds from his 32nd-floor suites in the Mandalay Bay hotel, killing sixty people and injuring 867, all attendees of the Route 91 Harvest country music festival. Paddock then turned his gun on himself. The event remains the deadliest mass shooting in modern American history.

I consulted *The Battle for Las Vegas* by Dennis N. Griffin[2] and *The Enforcer* by William F. Roemer, Jr.[3] for information on Spilotro, Cullotta, and the Chicago Outfit's stint in Las Vegas. The podcast "Mobbed Up"[4] was a further helpful resource on Cullotta—he's interviewed on the podcast—and especially on details of the Lisner murder. Martin Scorsese's 1995 film, *Casino*, also added color to my picture of Las Vegas's late-stage mob era.

Finally, many thanks to my editor, Heather Tekavec, my faithful readers of drafts, both early and late, and others who encouraged the project: Elliot Cooper, Chad Holley, David Noller, Scott Teems, and my comrades at the 2022 GoodLit Writers Retreat. This story would not exist without you.

---

1. Burbank, Jeff and Schumacher, Geoff. "EXCLUSIVE: Is THIS notorious mafia hitman Tony Spilotro the man behind Lake Mead's Mobster in the Barrel mystery? Mafia experts reveal tantalizing new link between killer who inspired Joe Pesci's role in Casino, three missing gangsters and Vegas reservoir." *DailyMail.com*, May 18, 2022. https://www.dailymail.co.uk/news/article-10829211/Vegas-mob-experts-reveal-link-Lake-Mead-MOBSTERS-BARREL-HITMAN.html. Accessed June 20, 2025.

2. Dennis N. Griffin. *The Battle for Las Vegas: The Law vs. the Mob* (Huntington Press, 2006).

3. William F. Roemer, Jr. *The Enforcer: Spilotro—The Chicago Mob's Man over Las Vegas* (Donald I. Fine, Inc., 1994).

4. Reed Redmond, *Mobbed Up: The Fight for Las Vegas*. Produced by The Las Vegas Review-Journal and The Mob Museum, 2020-2023, Podcast, MP3 audio, https://podcasts.apple.com/us/podcast/mobbed-up-the-fight-for-las-vegas/id1511810815

ABOUT THE AUTHOR

Aaron Mead is a writer of fiction and essays. His work has appeared in the *Los Angeles Times* and has been covered by National Public Radio. He lives with his family in the Los Angeles area.

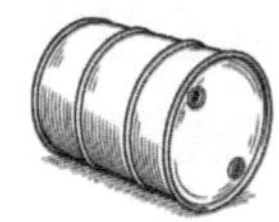

www.ameadwriter.com